D1014535

Word List

Here is a list of words that might make it easier to read this book. You'll find them in boldface the first time they appear in the story.

horizon	hor-EYE-zuhn
suspicious	suh-SPI-shuhs
orca	OR-kuh
quivering	QUI-ver-ing
dependent	di-PEN-duhnt
rascal	RAS-kuhl
hare	hair
gurgled	GER-guhld
kayak	KY-ak
dangerous	DAYN-jer-uhs
walrus	WALL-ruhs
gesture	JES-cher
interrupted	in-tuh-RUP-tid

Barbie™

A Sea of Friends

BARBIE and associated trademarks are owned by and used under license from Mattel, Inc. © 1998 Mattel, Inc. All Rights Reserved. Published by Grolier Books, a division of Grolier Enterprises, Inc. Story by Rita Balducci. Photo crew: Willy Lew, Susan Cracraft, Glen Bradley, Jeffrey Fiterman, and Judy Tsuno. Produced by Bumpy Slide Books. Printed in the United States of America.

ISBN: 0-7172-8825-0

GROLIER
B O O K S

The sun had just peeked out from behind a cloud. It made the waves around Barbie and her friends sparkle.

"I love sunny days," Barbie said with a sigh. She stretched out to float on her back in the warm water. Her tail shimmered in the sunshine.

"Me, too," agreed Teresa. She turned to Midge. "Don't you?" Teresa splashed Midge, who was shading her eyes.

"Not really. The sun hurts my eyes," Midge complained. "I don't know why you two make such a big deal about coming up to the surface."

Suddenly Barbie cried, "Look!"

Teresa spun around in the water as Midge dived out of sight. There on the **horizon** was a small boat.

"Let's get a closer look," Barbie said. With a gentle splash, she was off.

"Barbie, wait!" Teresa called after her. Up ahead she could see Barbie's head pop up and then duck down again as she got closer to the boat.

There was nothing Barbie loved more than watching humans up close. Most of the other mermaids were afraid of the world above the sea, but not Barbie. "Humans are just mermaids with legs," she would tell her friends.

Teresa quietly swam over to join Barbie. They swam under the boat and came up on the other side. A man sat on the deck, snoring. His hat was pulled down over his eyes, and he was holding a fishing pole. The fishing line was dangling in the water. Barbie winked at Teresa and gave the line a quick tug.

The man suddenly woke up. "Golly! I think I got a catch!" he shouted. But when he pulled the line in, there was nothing on the hook.

Barbie and Teresa dived under the water and giggled, sending up a stream of tiny bubbles.

The man leaned forward to look down into the water.

"Uh-oh, Teresa, he's **suspicious**!" Barbie said as she grabbed her friend's hand. Mermaids were not supposed to let people see them. The two dived deep and headed to their home beneath the waves.

"That was a close one," Barbie said when they were safely back home in their sea caves.

Barbie and Teresa were met by Midge and Barbie's sisters, Skipper, Stacie, and Kelly. All the mermaids glided through the water as gracefully as any fish. Each wore a crown of pearls in her long hair and beautiful seashell earrings.

"Barbie, where were you?" Skipper asked.

"Did you go to the surface again?"

"Oh, yes," said Barbie. Her voice was excited as she described the human she and Teresa had seen.

The young mermaids listened closely to everything Barbie said. They all laughed when Barbie told them about her teasing little tug on the fishing line.

"Tell us the story again," Stacie said with a twinkle in her eye.

As Barbie talked, Midge shook her head. "Mermaids belong down here," she said firmly when Barbie had finished. "We have nothing in common with humans."

Barbie thought about it for a moment. "It's true that humans are different from us. But we both have a lot in common with other living things. We *may* even be more alike than we think. Perhaps I will even talk to a human someday to find out!"

Midge gasped. "Oh, Barbie! You wouldn't!"

Barbie laughed at the shocked look on her

friend's face. "Oh, don't worry, Midge," she told her. "I don't run into humans that often, you know!"

Just then a squeal from Kelly made them turn around. The tiny mermaid was pointing to a large shadow passing overhead.

"Another boat?" Teresa asked, looking upward.

Barbie swam closer to the surface for a better look. Then she sang out a greeting. Her musical voice carried far through the water. The other mermaids listened, wondering whether there would be an answer.

There was! A voice sang back, then another. A third and then a fourth voice joined in. Soon the ocean was filled with happy singing.

"Who are they?" the mermaids asked when Barbie swam back to them.

Barbie smiled. "They're my friends the **orca** whales!" she explained. "I met them last year when I was exploring. They don't usually live around here. They must be passing through again on their way to somewhere else."

The mermaids listened to the happy orca family singing.

Then Midge nudged Barbie. "Mermaids and whales can sing, but I'll bet humans can't," she said. "They're probably too different from us."

Barbie thought that humans could sing. But she really didn't know if that was true. "I hope to find out one day!" she said to herself.

Chapter Two

Barbie quickly swam to meet the big, black-and-white whales. They remembered her.

"Barbie!" the whales cried together. "We hoped we would see you again!"

Barbie patted the side of a young whale named Oliver. "It's been a long time since you've been in this part of the ocean," she said.

The huge whale nodded. "Yes, it has," he said. "We're on our way back north."

"But why don't you just stay right here?" Barbie wanted to know.

"We can't," replied Oliver. "We go to the Far

North when it's summertime there. That's what whales have done for many, many years. And besides, it's an amazing place!"

Barbie wanted to hear all about it. "Tell me more," she begged.

"First we swim to the cold northern waters," the whale explained. "There we live with seals, polar bears, and other animals. Sometimes, at night, shimmering, colorful lights appear in the sky. You've never seen anything like it!"

Barbie shook her head. "No, I don't think I ever have," she replied. "But I would love to someday."

"Hey! Why not come with us now?" Oliver suggested.

Barbie thought for a moment. "Oh, I'd really love to," she said to Oliver. "But there's my family to think about. I'll have to talk this over with them."

"Okay, we'll be here resting for a little while

longer," the whale replied. "I'm sure my family wouldn't mind waiting for you."

Without wasting a minute, Barbie swam off to her sea cave. She told everyone about Oliver's invitation. All of the mermaids were very excited for Barbie.

"Of course you should go," said Teresa. She turned to Skipper. "You'll help me watch Stacie and Kelly, right?"

"No problem," said Skipper, swishing her tail.

"We'll miss you, Sis," said Stacie. "But it sounds like a lot of fun!"

"Barbie go bye-bye?" asked Kelly.

Barbie hugged all of her sisters and gave them each a kiss. "I'll miss all of you," Barbie told them. "But I promise I'll come back soon."

"I say you belong right here with us," Midge said. "Who knows what might happen to you so far away from home?"

Barbie gave her friend a hug. "I'll be all right,"

she said. "I know how to take care of myself. Besides, I have some pretty big friends to protect me. I really have to go now. Oliver's waiting."

"Who's Oliver?" Midge asked in confusion. But Barbie was already off in a cloud of bubbles.

The whales were waiting for her at the surface. Fountains of steam and water shot into the air from the blowholes on the tops of their heads. They nodded a friendly hello to Barbie.

"I'm ready to go," Barbie said. Then they all set off together.

The whales were strong, fast swimmers. They invited Barbie to hang onto their fins so she wouldn't get tired. As they sped through the water, Barbie noticed differences in the ocean the farther north they went. Little by little, the water became colder.

After a few days, Barbie asked Oliver, "Are we in the Far North yet?"

"I think so," the young orca replied. "When we see the seals we'll know we're there."

Barbie was about to ask what seals look like when she heard a high whistle from the whale leading the group.

"Welcome home, everyone!" he cried.

Excitement spread throughout the group. Barbie watched as the whales swam in circles, diving down deep and then leaping up out of the water. They fell hard on their backs with a splash! Barbie giggled as she was sprayed with cold water. She pulled herself out of the water and sat on a large rock to look around.

Just then she heard a little voice cry, "Hello!"

Barbie turned to see two huge, round, black eyes shining at her. Stiff whiskers poked out on either side of a **quivering** nose. The roly-poly little animal was covered with soft, white fur that shone in the sunshine.

"What are you?" the animal asked Barbie.

"I'm a mermaid," Barbie replied with a smile. "I was hoping to see a seal. I've never

seen one before."

"I *am* a seal! My name is Dawn!" the seal pup shouted happily. Then she began swimming and spinning in the water. Barbie laughed as she watched the playful little pup. She had made a new friend already.

Chapter Three

The days in the northern sea were great fun. Every day Barbie met new and wonderful creatures of the North. She sang silly seal songs with Dawn and her family. She also played with her old friends the orca whales. Together, they sang and splashed in the waves as the summer months passed.

"Thank you so much for bringing me with you," Barbie said to Oliver one day. "You've made me feel like one of your family."

The whale spouted water as he answered. "Life in the Far North can be hard sometimes.

Some animal families come here to feed. Others come to raise their babies. But we are all **dependent** on one another. And we all must live together, whether we are whales or eagles or seals."

"Speaking of seals," Barbie began, "I promised Dawn I would teach her some mermaid songs today."

"Good luck!" the orca snorted. Then he splashed away to join some other friends.

"Now, where can that little **rascal** be?" Barbie wondered as she swam over to the shore. There were dozens of sweet, furry baby seals there, but Dawn was nowhere to be seen. Then Barbie spotted Dawn's mother. Barbie asked her if she knew where Dawn was.

"I was just about to go look for her," Dawn's mother said. "I think she went exploring again. And it's time for that little seal's nap!"

"Would you like me to find her for you?" Barbie asked the seal mother. "Then I could put her down for her nap."

"That would be wonderful," replied Dawn's mother. "That way, I could go catch some fish for Dawn's lunch." The seal mother waved as she swam away.

"I hope Dawn didn't go too far," Barbie thought. When she didn't spot the pup along the coast, Barbie decided to swim inland, up a narrow seaway.

The seaway wound past high cliffs lined with tall pine trees. In the distance were tall mountains capped with snow. Barbie could see eagles soaring overhead. On the shore, she spotted a **hare** that was dashing into the tall grass.

Just then, Barbie saw a splash of water behind some rocks on the shoreline. When she swam over, she was glad to see Dawn. The little seal was playing happily in a tiny, hidden pool of water.

"There you are!" Barbie called. "I'm afraid

it's time for you to go home for your nap, young lady. The mermaid songs will just have to wait until tomorrow."

Dawn swam back with Barbie to the coast. Once Dawn was safely settled on a rock in the sun to take her nap, Barbie headed back to the seaway. It was beautiful there, and she wanted to do some exploring of her own. Dawn's mother would be back shortly.

Barbie swam farther and farther up the seaway. Around her the cold water **gurgled** merrily over rocks on its way to the open sea. The wind sighed softly through the pine trees on the cliffs. Then Barbie heard a strange new sound.

Clear, sweet notes of singing filled the air. It was not the singing of a bird or a whale or another mermaid. Barbie had never heard anything like it. She swam toward the sound.

To her surprise, the singing voice belonged to a human. It was a young woman paddling a small, narrow boat. She had long, black hair and almond-shaped eyes. The woman's song told of long summer days and long winter nights and of shimmering lights in the sky. Barbie listened, and without thinking, she joined in the singing.

The young woman stopped singing and paddling when she heard Barbie's voice. She sat up straight, listening. Barbie ducked just below the water's surface. She could still see the woman.

"Who's there?" the human called out.

Barbie bit her lip. She wanted so much to answer! She had always dreamed of meeting a real, live human, and here was one calling to her! But then she thought of Midge and all her warnings. Maybe humans really were too different from mermaids. Maybe they really were not to be trusted.

Just then two whales rose up from the water and came crashing down beside Barbie. They were Oliver and his brother.

"Hi, Barbie!" the shiny whales called as they continued on their way.

Barbie turned around quickly to look for the woman. Then she finally spotted her. The woman was in the water, and the **kayak** was floating upside down beside her. The waves made by the whales had turned the boat over.

The young woman quickly flipped her kayak right-side up and climbed back in. Then she seemed to be looking around for something.

Barbie jumped as something nudged her side. The mermaid had never seen anything like it. It looked like two fins attached to a long stick, floating in the water.

"The woman must need this to make her boat go," Barbie thought. She decided she would help this human with the beautiful voice. Besides, she might never get the chance to meet a human again!

Barbie ducked under the water, pushing the

20

paddle toward the boat. She was nervous about finally meeting a human, but she was excited, too. "It's now or never," she said to herself.

Barbie rose to the surface of the water. She held out the paddle in front of her.

The young woman had turned her back and was looking for the paddle on the other side of the boat. Barbie made a little splash with her tail to get the woman's attention.

The woman spun around and gasped. The human and the mermaid were looking right at each other!

Chapter Four

Suddenly Barbie got scared. What if Midge was right about humans? The mermaid was just about to dive as deep as she could when the young woman spoke.

"Wait! Please don't go!" she cried. "At least let me thank you for finding my paddle!"

Barbie stopped. This human did not seem **dangerous.** Barbie smiled. "You're welcome," she said shyly. "My name is Barbie."

The woman smiled back. "I'm Eva," she said. "You saved me from drifting out to sea!"

"Oh, I would never have let you get lost at

sea," Barbie said. "Although, with a voice like yours, you could be a great mermaid."

"I thought that's what you were," Eva whispered. "I've heard of mermaids, but most people think they're make-believe. Was that you singing with me?"

Barbie moved closer. "Yes," she replied, "until my friends knocked over your boat. Sorry about that."

"Those big whales are friends of yours?" Eva asked. "How much fun that must be! Tell me what it's like to live in the sea."

"I'll tell you, if you tell me what it's like to live on land," Barbie said. "You are the first human I've ever spoken to."

"Well, you're the first mermaid *anyone* has ever spoken to, I think," Eva said, "unless I'm dreaming! Maybe that dunk in the cold water is making me see things!"

They both laughed.

Then Eva began to tell Barbie about herself. She spoke of her brothers and sisters and her parents and grandparents. She told Barbie about their snug home made of earth and wood. Eva confessed, "My family is always telling me I daydream too much."

Barbie giggled. "Your family sounds like my family," she said. "They tell me I'm a dreamer, too." Then Barbie told Eva about life under the sea.

"You know, we're a lot alike," Eva said when Barbie was finished. Eva thought about it and chuckled to herself. "Except, of course, you have a tail and I don't. Why do you think people and mermaids haven't met before?"

Barbie sighed. "Most mermaids are afraid of people," she told Eva. "They hear of humans in boats who hunt their whale friends. They see trash dumped in the water. They hear seagulls talk about places where all the fish are dying." Barbie stopped.

She was afraid of hurting her new friend's feelings.

"I know," Eva said gently. "All of that is true. The oceans are different from our homes on land. And some humans don't know how to treat things that are different."

"But there are many people, like me, who love the earth and all of its animals," Eva went on. "Living things in the sea are different from us, but they should be respected. I think it's important to learn how others live." Eva thought for a moment, then smiled. "That's how we make new friends," she said.

Barbie smiled back. She wanted to ask Eva a million questions, but she noticed that the woman had begun to shiver.

"Are you cold?" Barbie asked. Mermaids weren't bothered by the cold, but Barbie had heard that humans were.

Eva shivered again. "Yes. I wish I could stay and talk longer, but I have to go home and dry off.

I wasn't planning on taking a swim today!"

"Your boat is out pretty far from the shore," Barbie told Eva. Then she offered to help Eva get back to land.

Barbie swam alongside the kayak and pushed it as Eva paddled. When they reached land, Eva leapt ashore. She pulled the lightweight boat out of the water. For a moment, Barbie wondered what it would be like to jump and stand like that.

"Well," Eva said slowly, "thank you for helping me today. I hate to leave. It's been so much fun talking to you, Barbie."

"I've enjoyed talking to you, too," Barbie said. "But I think it would be better if we kept our meeting a secret. Others might not think it's a good thing that we talked."

"I won't tell anyone," Eva promised. "No one would believe me, anyway. If I started talking about mermaids, my family would never let me out of the house again!"

The two new friends laughed out loud.

Then Eva grew serious. "Barbie," she said, "I don't live far from here. If you ever need me, just come to this place and sing. I will come find you."

Barbie smiled. "Thank you," she said.

Eva lifted the kayak onto her shoulder and waved good-bye. Then she turned and walked into the woods. Barbie sat on a rock watching her go. She wondered what it might be like to walk.

Chapter Five

As Barbie swam back to the open ocean, her mind was racing with all the things she had learned that afternoon. She hoped she would see Eva again sometime.

"Barbie!" called a voice from across the waves. "Thank goodness you're back!"

Barbie quickly swam over to a big **walrus,** named Walter, who was waving to her. He was very upset. "What's the matter?" she asked.

"It's Dawn," the walrus told Barbie. "No one has seen her since she woke up from her nap. The seals have been searching for her all afternoon!

Have you seen her?"

"No," Barbie said. "But she likes to go exploring, and it will be dark soon. We have to find her!"

"Come on!" the walrus called, diving into the water.

Barbie and Walter found the worried seals gathered on Seal Rock. Some seagulls were nearby, and so was Barbie's whale friend, Oliver.

"Is there anything we can do, Barbie?" asked a seagull.

Barbie could see that the animals were looking to her for help. She quickly took charge.

"Seals, you search the tidal pool by Polar Bay. Dawn likes to play there. Oliver and Walter, you spread the word to all the fish to be on the lookout for her. Seagulls, fly over the cliffs and see if you can spot Dawn from up high," Barbie directed them.

"What about me?" called a timid voice from

the shoreline. "I'd like to help, too."

Barbie looked over her shoulder. There, at the edge of the water, was a furry little hare. He sat up and tried to look very brave.

"You hop along the shoreline. See if Dawn is playing there," Barbie told him. In an instant, the hare was off.

"Barbie, what if humans have caught Dawn?" asked the baby seal's mother. "Everyone says they are very mean."

Barbie put her arms around the worried mother. "Not all humans are bad," she told her. "Besides, Dawn has probably just wandered too far and is waiting for us to find her."

The mother seal smiled at Barbie. "I hope you're right," she said.

"I hope so, too," Barbie thought. "But what if I'm wrong?" Then she announced, "I'm going back up the seaway. Dawn was there today. Maybe she went back."

Everyone went off to search. With her heart pounding, Barbie set off to find Dawn, too.

Barbie swam as fast as she could. The light was fading as she neared the spot where she had met Eva.

The soft glow of a light up ahead caught Barbie's attention. It was the lantern of a fishing boat. The boat rocked gently in the icy water, and Barbie saw two people. They were hauling a heavy net into the boat. The woman reached into the net for something. That something was small and white. It was Dawn!

Barbie watched as the man took off his parka and wrapped it around the little seal. The woman offered Dawn a fish from the net, but the baby didn't eat it.

"Poor little Dawn," thought Barbie. "She looks tired, and I'll bet she's scared, too."

Barbie swam closer to the boat. "Eva was nice," she thought. "Perhaps I'll be able to talk to these humans."

But the man put the oars into the water and began rowing toward the shore.

"Wait!" Barbie called. But the wind carried her voice away. The boat quickly disappeared into the growing darkness.

Chapter Six

Barbie ducked underwater and raced after the boat. She lifted her head now and then to keep the lantern in sight.

When the boat reached the shore, Barbie watched as the man quickly jumped out. Then he held his arms out to the woman. She climbed out of the boat, carefully holding the bundle close to her body. Her boots crunched along the shore as she hurried up a path into the woods. The man followed.

Barbie's heart sank. She knew she had to find them. But how? If only she had legs and could follow them on land!

Suddenly Barbie thought of Eva. Eva had said that if Barbie ever needed her, she would be there to help.

There was no time to lose. With the stars as her guide, Barbie swam quickly to the rocky spot where she had said good-bye to Eva that afternoon.

"Eva!" Barbie sang out, her voice like a bell. "I need your help!"

There was a fluttering sound as birds flew out of a nearby tree. Barbie waited for a moment, but there was no answer from her friend.

"Eva!" she sang again. Then she listened. She heard the water lapping at the shore, and she heard the hoot of an owl. Then she heard footsteps.

"Barbie?" called Eva's voice.

Eva ran down to the shore, her long hair flying behind her. There was a look of concern on her face.

"Barbie, is that you?" she called out.

"Eva!" cried Barbie.

"What's wrong?" Eva asked.

"I need your help," Barbie told her. "My friend Dawn has been caught by people in a fishing boat, not far from here. She's a baby seal."

"Oh, no!" gasped Eva.

"I followed the boat to shore and saw a man and a woman carry her away," continued Barbie. "Can you help me find her?"

"Don't worry about anything," Eva told Barbie. "Whoever took Dawn is probably trying to protect her from harm. I'm sure your little friend is all right."

"I believe you," Barbie said. Still, she knew she would feel a lot better once Dawn was back with her own family.

Then Eva had an idea. "My kayak is nearby," she told Barbie. "Why don't you lead me to the place where you saw the boat land? Then I'll go ashore to find the baby seal."

"That sounds great," said Barbie. "Let's go!"

Eva ran into the woods and quickly returned with her kayak. She put it in the water and climbed in. Then the two friends were off, with Barbie leading the way farther up the seaway.

Soon Barbie spotted the fishing boat tied on the bank.

"There's the boat, Eva!" Barbie cried.

Eva stopped paddling and peered into the darkness. Then she let out a happy whoop. "Everything is going to be fine, Barbie!" she said. "That boat belongs to my Uncle Jake and Aunt Leota. And their home is nearby."

Barbie waited at the edge of the water as Eva scrambled ashore. The cabin was close to the water, and Barbie could see the front door. As Eva hurried up the path, the door opened. A woman stepped out. Behind her was a man with a large basket strapped to his back. Barbie recognized the man and woman as the people from the boat.

"Aunt Leota! Uncle Jake!" said Eva.

The man and woman greeted Eva warmly.

"How fortunate! We were just on our way to find you," Aunt Leota said.

"We need your help," Uncle Jake said. "Look what we found!" He took the basket from his back and placed it gently on the ground. Barbie's heart leapt as she watched.

Eva knelt down and gently pulled back the blanket covering the basket. Two huge, round, black eyes shone up at her from inside.

"Well, hello!" Eva cried, reaching in to stroke Dawn's soft head.

"She was tangled in our fishing net when we pulled it in this evening," Uncle Jake explained. "We don't know where she belongs, but we knew it wasn't safe just to let her go, alone. We tried to feed her some dried fish, and we were about to bring her to you."

"Eva, you know what to do, don't you?"

Aunt Leota asked. "You spend so much time with all those whales and seals, you're almost like one of them yourself."

"That's right," Uncle Jake said with a laugh. "Half human, half fish!"

"You mean like a mermaid?" Eva joked.

By the shore, Barbie giggled, covering her mouth with her hand.

Eva grew serious. "You were right not to leave this pup," she told her aunt and uncle. "I saw some seals when I was kayaking today. Perhaps she belongs with them."

Dawn poked her head out of the basket and nuzzled Eva's hand. She seemed to know that she was among friends.

Then Eva smiled and hugged her aunt and uncle good-bye.

Aunt Leota peeked into the basket. "Good-bye, little one!" she said.

"Good-bye," said Eva to her aunt and uncle.

"I'll take care of her."

Eva strapped the basket to her back and hurried back to the shore, where Barbie was waiting.

Barbie was thrilled to see Dawn's bright little face poking out of the basket.

"Oh, Dawn!" Barbie exclaimed.

The baby seal was happy to see her, too, and tried to wriggle out.

"Okay, okay," Eva said, laughing. She knelt down so Dawn could climb out of the basket.

With a splash, the little seal was in the water with Barbie. Then she barked loudly, "I want my mama!"

"She wants you, too," Barbie said. "Let's go!"

The two began to swim away, but then Barbie stopped. She turned to Eva, who was still standing on the shore.

"Aren't you coming?" Barbie asked. "The animals will be so happy to have Dawn back safely. I know they'll want to thank you."

Eva was touched by Barbie's thoughtful **gesture.** "I'd love to join you," she said quickly. Then she steadied her kayak in the water, climbed in, and pushed away from the shore.

Chapter Seven

The animals had gathered once again at Seal Rock. The seagulls had told them that Dawn was trapped by a fisherman's net. Now everyone wondered whether they would ever see the baby seal again.

"I hope Barbie hasn't been captured, too," said a seal.

Oliver snorted at the idea. "Don't be silly!" the whale said. "Barbie is far too smart to ever get captured!" But deep down, everyone was worried.

Just then a shout came from one of the seals. "Here comes Barbie! And she's not alone!"

The animals all hurried to one side of the rock to see Barbie. They were all very excited to see that Dawn was with her. And they were *very* surprised to see a human in a little boat, following right behind Barbie and Dawn!

"Dawn!" cried the baby seal's mother, leaping into the water.

"Mama!" shouted Dawn, racing to her mother's side.

The animals all splashed into the water to surround little Dawn. They were overjoyed to have her home safely at last.

"Oh, Barbie!" cried the mother seal. "How can we ever thank you for bringing Dawn back home to us, safe and sound?"

"It wasn't just me," said Barbie. "My friend Eva helped rescue Dawn, and so did her aunt and uncle."

A hush fell over the animals as they all looked at Eva. They had always been afraid of human beings. After all, people were so *different!* But if Barbie thought this human was a friend, perhaps some of the differences didn't really matter, after all.

"Hooray for Eva and her aunt and uncle! Hip-hip-hooray!" cried the walruses.

The animals pushed Eva's kayak to Seal Rock. The young woman got out amid cheers from all her new animal friends. Barbie winked at her as she joined Eva on the rock.

Suddenly Eva called, "Look! The northern lights!"

Everyone looked up to see the shimmering lights. Ribbons of red, yellow, blue, pink, and green lights danced across the sky like silent fireworks.

"At last!" Barbie cried. She had waited so long to see the northern lights, and they were even more wonderful than she had imagined. But suddenly she felt a tiny bit homesick. If only her sisters and friends could be with her to see the

beautiful sight, too.

Her thoughts were **interrupted** by Eva. "I have to say good-bye, Barbie," the woman said. "I love being with all your animal friends, but it's time I went home. My family will be missing me."

"I hope I will see you again someday, and maybe even meet your family," Barbie told her.

Eva smiled. "I would like that," she said. "Perhaps your family and mermaid friends will all come north one summer!"

Barbie nodded happily. "I know they'll want to when I tell them about my visit here," she said.

Eva climbed into her kayak. She waved farewell as she paddled off, and Barbie and the animals waved back.

"It's time I was leaving, too, Oliver," Barbie said. "I've had a wonderful time here. I can't wait to tell everyone back home all about it!"

Chapter Eight

The next morning, Barbie said good-bye to the seals, the walruses, and the whales. Then she said a special good-bye to Dawn.

"I'll miss you," Dawn said shyly.

Barbie gave the little seal a hug. Barbie knew she would miss all her new friends, but she promised to return, bringing her sisters and friends with her.

As everyone called out farewells, Barbie set off south. The journey home took longer by herself. She had to stop now and then to rest.

But after several days, the water began to get

warmer. The sun was stronger here than in the North. She had almost forgotten how nice warm weather could be!

The kinds of sea creatures she met changed, too. Playful dolphins leapt out of the water, twisting and turning in the air.

"Show-offs!" called Barbie, teasing them.

Some seagulls Barbie recognized flew overhead. "Where have you been, Barbie?" they called. "We've missed you!"

Barbie searched the horizon for signs of home. All she could see ahead of her were the little white-capped ocean waves and the bright blue sky. But then something else appeared in the distance. It was a tiny island that Barbie remembered. She dived underwater. Some familiar coral rocks lay beneath her. She was almost home!

"Barbie!" called a voice in the distance.

It was Barbie's friend Teresa. "Hey, everyone! Barbie's back!"

Barbie was tired but she didn't care. She swam even faster. Her sisters were racing to meet her. Not far behind them were Midge and Teresa.

"Hi, everyone!" Barbie cried as she reached them. "Wow, Stacie, you're so much bigger! And Skipper, it's so good to see you! Kelly, are those seashells for me?"

Barbie was happy to be surrounded by her loved ones once again. It had been a while since she had seen them all, and she had so much to tell them about her visit to the Far North.

The mermaids linked arms and headed for home. They sang as they swam, because that is what mermaids do when they are happy.

Later on, Barbie began telling everyone about her adventures.

"But Barbie, didn't you miss us at all?" Stacie asked. "We sure missed you here."

"Of course I did!" Barbie cried. "I often thought how much nicer it would have been if all of you were with me!"

Midge shook her head in confusion. "But everything must have been so different," she said.

Barbie smiled. "Some of it was," she agreed.

Then Barbie went on with her story. She talked about the orcas, the walruses, Dawn and her mother, and, finally, Eva and her family. Then everyone was quiet.

"Wow!" said Midge at last. "I never knew a human could be so much like a mermaid."

Barbie nodded. "Mermaids, humans, and other animals are all very different. But in our love for our family and friends, we are all very much the same."